Over the Sea to Skye

First published in 1997 by Franklin Watts

This paperback edition published in 1998

Franklin Watts
96 Leonard Street
London EC2A 4RH

Franklin Watts Australia
14 Mars Road
Lane Cove
NSW 2006

Editor: Kyla Barber
Series editor: Paula Borton
Designer: Kirstie Billingham
Consultant: Douglas Ansdell

A CIP catalogue record for this book
is available from the British Library.

ISBN   0 7496 3126 0 (pbk)
       0 7496 2588 0 (hbk)

Dewey Classification 941.107

Printed in Great Britain

Over the Sea to Skye

by
Kirsty White

Illustrations by Martin Remphry

W

FRANKLIN WATTS
LONDON • NEW YORK • SYDNEY

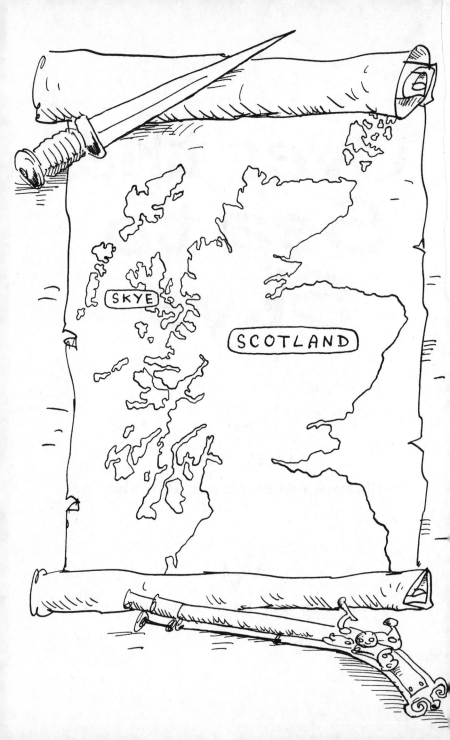

1

A Call to Battle

Robby was bored and frustrated. He wished he was old enough to go with the men and fight for Bonnie Prince Charlie.

The Great Hall was full of women worrying, so he slipped down to the dungeons beneath the castle where, in the old days,

his ancestors had held their enemies
prisoner.

The dungeons had not been used for
years and the bolts on the doors had rusted
away. Robby waited until his eyes adjusted
to the gloom then he looked around and
saw, in a corner, a pile of plaids. After the
rising began there'd been a story that the
Redcoats had orders to shoot on sight
anyone wearing a kilt, so his mother had

made the boys wear trews instead. Robby
felt silly in trews. Almost as silly as he felt
speaking English.

He picked up a plaid and put it on and
then stood proudly to attention, imagining
that he faced King George's army. Robby
held his arm out, one foot forward, waving
a make-believe sword. "Hee-ugh!" he
roared as he lunged forward.

The floor was slippery. Robby slid and

fell, landing with a thud on his bottom.
Winded, he lay there for a moment. As he
got up, he noticed a dull gleam beneath
the plaids. He pushed them aside and
found some rusty old claymores and a
pair of shields.

"Robby?" Neil, his younger brother,
called from the top of the stairs.

"Ssshh," Robby hissed. "Look what I've found."

Neil picked up a claymore. The two-edged sword was as long as he was tall, and so heavy that he could barely lift it.

"You be a Sassenach, I'll be Charlie," Robby said.

"Not here. They'll hear us."

The brothers picked up a claymore and shield each and crept out of the castle. They began to practise sword fighting in the meadow beyond the wall.

Meanwhile their sister Maggie wandered through the castle, looking for her brothers. With the war so close, she was worried that they'd get into trouble.

For weeks there'd been rumours that Prince Charles Edward Stuart's army was facing defeat. The day before, a man wearing Cameron tartan had cantered into the stable yard and rushed straight into the castle. The powerful Cameron clan were Bonnie Prince Charlie's most loyal supporters.

"You must send help," he said to Maggie's father, the chief of the MacDonnells of Glenaffin. "We need more men."

The chief did not reply and a tremor of fear passed through Maggie.

The chief paced the floor, as he always did when he was worried. The clan had gone to fight for Charlie, but they'd come home when the campaign began to falter months before.

"Where's Charlie now?" the chief asked.

"In Nairn. The Sassenachs are headed for Inverness."

The chief cursed. "If Charlie'd stayed in Edinburgh it'd be all over by now."

The messenger looked Maggie's father in the eye. "You'd not desert the cause?" he said.

"Of course not!" the chief replied. "I'll give you all the help I can."

Maggie's stomach tightened. Abruptly, her father gave the order to round up his men. They would leave as soon as the horses were ready. There was no time to delay.

"You're not going?" her mother asked him. The chief had been badly injured when, as a lad, he'd joined the previous rising of thirty years before.

"Of course I am," he said tersely. "I'd not ask my men to do something I'd not do myself."

"But your arm, you can't . . ."

"I have to, woman," he said in a voice that told Maggie he would discuss it no further.

When the rising began, there'd been high hopes for Prince Charlie – his army had defeated King George's at the Battle of Prestonpans. But when Charlie invaded England the tide of war turned, and Charlie's army was now on the run.

Maggie walked out into the sunlight. Robby and Neil weren't in the castle. She smiled when she saw them playing in the meadow. They held the heavy swords like pokers, prodding at each other. In the end Neil gave up his sword and shoved Robby with his shield, knocking him to the ground.

Robby roared with anger as Neil stood over him yelling, "You're dead!"

"That's not fair," Robby protested. "You're not supposed to push me over."

"Of course it's fair," Neil insisted. "If we'd been in battle, you'd be dead!"

Maggie stopped smiling at the thought of her brother lying bleeding on a battlefield. Neil looked at her, expecting her to take his side in the argument as she usually did.

"Isn't that right?" Neil said.

She shook her head. "Nothing's right about war, Neil. No good comes from killing people."

Neil said nothing. Robby frowned at her. "They're our enemies. You have to kill your enemies."

"If you kill your enemies," Maggie said, "then you make enemies of their friends and they'll kill you. It'll go on and on until everyone's dead. You know what Uncle Lachie said. The Redcoats were pretty decent to him."

"Oh, Redcoats are decent now, are they? What were they doing at Glencoe?" demanded Robby.

There was no answer to that.

2

Loyal to the Cause

Maggie knew that Robby and Neil blamed her for spoiling their game. She went back indoors, feeling cold despite the sun.

With all the men gone to fight for Charlie the castle was silent and tension filled the air. Maggie went to sit in the

library. Normally the room was cheerful,
with a big fire and candles, but today
nobody had lit the fire and Maggie didn't
bother to light the candles. She just sat there
in the dark, thinking and worrying.

She remembered her joy when her father
had raised his glass to James VIII,
Prince Charlie's father, newly proclaimed
king in Edinburgh the year before.

"Things'll get better now," he'd said, happily. "It'll be like old times again."

His mood changed when he heard that James had been proclaimed king of England, Ireland and France as well.

"What?" her father ranted. "Isn't one country enough for him?"

"Ach," Lachie, Maggie's great-uncle, said, "the lad's got as much right to be king of England as that wee Georgie had to be king of us."

Despite her worry, Maggie smiled when she thought of Lachie. He was the oldest man of the clan, rumoured to be at least ninety, though he boasted himself that he was over a hundred. Lachie had fought for the Stuarts at Killiecrankie nearly sixty years before, and plotted gleefully in all the risings since then. He'd been furious when her father had told him firmly that he was too old to fight for Charlie.

"Ach, Lachie," the chief had said, "you're past it, man."

Lachie hadn't given up without a fight. The chief had to take him out on a deer hunt before he managed to convince Lachie that he couldn't see well enough to shoot straight.

"I could give him moral support," Lachie said.

"Away, man. You can do that here!"

The chief was furious when he'd heard about the invasion of England, but Lachie had just nodded and said that Charlie might

have bitten off more than he could chew.

The clansmen sent a message home saying that they were hungry and that the Prince's generals didn't know what they were doing. The chief thought about it sadly before sending a reply telling them to come home if they thought that it was the best thing for them to do. They could always rejoin the army if Charlie's generals came to their senses.

As she remembered it all, Maggie heard the old man's cane tap-tapping along the stone passage. Catching sight of the dejected girl, Lachie came in and sat down beside her.

"You're worried, pet," he said.

"What else can I do?"

He smiled. "Worrying doesn't help. I was just wondering if I should volunteer for the Redcoats again."

Maggie burst out laughing at the thought
of what happened the last time Lachie
volunteered.

Just after her father had told his men
to come home, a Redcoat officer from Fort
William appeared with an order for the
chief. He was required to send men to join King
George's army. Maggie thought that her father

would explode.

"I don't believe the cheek of it," the chief raved.

"Ach," Lachie said, "where's your manners? We have to feed the messenger laddie at least."

At dinner Lachie made sure that the Redcoat's glass was always full of the special whisky that he distilled himself. When the Redcoat fell into a stupor, Lachie grinned.

"Now, we can decide what to do with him," he said as they left the dinner table.

The chief began to rant again.

"MacDonnells fight for the Usurper? The man must be crazy."

Lachie said nothing. Maggie just waited. Her brothers had been sent to bed, but in his rage her father had forgotten her.

"You'll have to do something," Maggie's mother said. "Send a few men at least."

"Over my dead body," the chief roared.

Meanwhile the soldier slept soundly, snoring loudly.

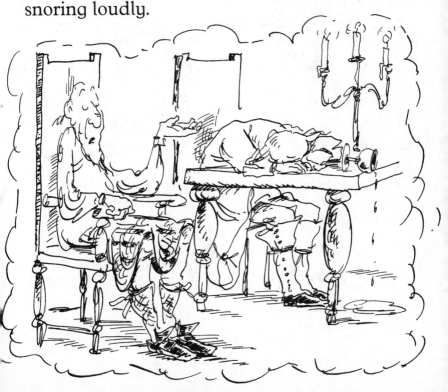

"I'll not do it," the chief said.

"You have to," his wife insisted.

"I'll away and fight for them," Lachie said quietly.

Maggie remembered her surprise. If anyone was for the Stuarts, it was Lachie. He'd always refused to raise his glass to King George in company, even at the risk of being denounced as a rebel.

Lachie said he was too old to be scared of the daft Sassenach laws.

"Don't be ridiculous," the chief said. "You'd be more of a hindrance than a help."

"Exactly," Lachie said, winking at Maggie.

The following day, Lachie set off, leading a band of men that the chief was sending to King George's army. He took his friends, all men over sixty.

They carried sticks and spades, because
King George's laws forbade clansmen to
bear weapons. Lachie had waved jauntily
at Maggie as they left, saying that they'd
be back in no time.

Lachie was as good as his word. They
all came back just after Christmas,
boasting about having been discharged on

medical grounds. They'd been appointed as cooks to the army, but they'd managed to spoil every single meal.

"I still have my red coat," Lachie said now, grinning at Maggie.

Maggie shook her head. Lachie and his men had even purloined uniforms from King George's army.

"I was wondering if we could distract them," Lachie added mischievously.

Maggie laughed. Lachie had managed to cheer her up, as he always did.

Over dinner he told funny stories about all the food he had ruined for the army.

As Maggie got up to go to bed, Lachie patted her hand.

"Don't fret, pet," he said. "Your father's as wise as he's brave. No harm will come to him and his men."

"I'll try not to," she said.

"Promise?"

"Promise."

Despite her promise, Maggie couldn't help worrying. She could not get to sleep.

3

The Battle is Over

In the small hours, Maggie heard the
sound of horses. She got up and peered out
of the tiny window. There, in the distance,
she saw the chief returning with the rest of
the men. Maggie was thrilled that they
were safely home.

She ran downstairs to meet him. He smiled
gently and ruffled her hair and said that she
should have trusted him. But the other men
weren't smiling and the chief's face soon
turned grave again.

As Maggie climbed the stairs, she heard the
men talking about the terrible defeat that
Charlie had suffered at Drummossie. They'd

only escaped by sheer luck.

Maggie was terribly sad, but she was glad that her father and the other clansmen were safe. Lachie said it was Charlie's own fault for listening to the wrong advice, and he had only himself to blame.

Back in bed, Maggie slept.

In the morning, a messenger came with news that the Redcoats were everywhere, searching for Charlie and anyone else who had survived the slaughter. The chief ordered his men to hide, then he posted sentries on the castle roof to watch out for soldiers. Robby and Neil went up there too, vowing to shoot the Sassenach on sight. Maggie looked on, with a heavy heart. Her brothers were too young to understand what defeat meant.

Inside the castle everyone was talking about what had happened. Despite all the

Prince's faults, the clan still supported him, and were greatly saddened by his defeat. Maggie decided to go out for a ride to get away from the sense of despair.

"Be careful," her father said as she set off.

Avoiding the track that ran alongside the river, Maggie rode towards the hills. She went through the broom that was just beginning to flower yellow and then into the forest that lined the edge of the glen.

She rode for hours along the path that threaded its way through the trees. When the sun reached its mid-point in the sky she stopped, thinking that it was time to turn back.

Maggie heard the sound then, a rustling in the grass as if she had disturbed a deer.

She waited, hardly daring to breathe, until she saw, through the trees, a flash of tartan. She called out in Gaelic, relieved that it wasn't a Redcoat. The branches parted and a man stood there, clad in Cameron tartan. He carried a sword and also a rifle.

"Are you loyal?" he asked her.

"I'll help if I can," she said, seeing the white cockade pinned to his beret.

The man said something in English, she didn't catch what, and the branches parted again. A second man stepped out. He was slim and young with dark hair tied in a pony tail. He was clad haphazardly in breeches and a shirt, with a plaid slung around his shoulders.

Maggie gazed into the man's eyes and knew that this was Prince Charlie.

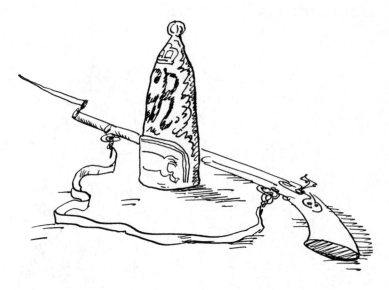

4

A Prince in Danger

"We've come from Drummossie," the clansman said. "Loch Eil's not safe – there's too many Redcoats."

Maggie nodded. "Where are you headed?"

"If we can reach Skye, there's a chance the Prince can escape."

"I'll take you to the Sound of Sleat. It's our land. You'll be safe."

The Prince's eyes were heavy with exhaustion. Maggie dismounted and handed him the reins of her horse. He got on meekly.

"There are more behind us, trying to lay a false trail for the Redcoats," the clansman said.

"We'll go to the castle," Maggie said. "My father will help."

The clansman drew her to one side. "They weren't at Drummossie?"

"The message came too late. They'd left before the battle started."

The clansman shook his head. "They were fortunate," he said.

When they reached the edge of the forest, Maggie crept forward. There was a silence that she didn't like. Even the birds had stopped singing.

She looked down and saw that the castle was surrounded by Redcoats.

"Stay here," she told the clansman. "I'll try to head them off."

He grasped her arm. "Can we trust you?"

"Of course," Maggie said. She was insulted that he even asked.

Maggie left her companions at the edge of the forest and ran towards the castle. A tall, wiry Redcoat soldier stepped out and barred her way.

"Halt!" the Redcoat roared in English. "Who are you?"

Maggie smiled at him, "I'm MacDonnell's daughter. I'm just coming back from a walk."

He stood aside and Maggie strode past him with her nose in the air.

Only her father knew that she had left on horseback. Only he would wonder why she had returned on foot.

Robby and Neil were sitting on the steps that led to the door.

"They say Charlie's hiding somwhere nearby. We're going to help!" Neil whispered. Maggie thought quickly. She needed to distract the Redcoats, but she didn't want Robby or Neil to get hurt.

"Why don't you keep an eye on the Redcoats instead?" she said.

Robby's face fell but Neil grinned.

"Yes!" he said. "We'll be spies!"

In the Great Hall, the chief was talking

to two Redcoat officers. He was explaining to them how the clan had been loyal to the Usurper and waved Lachie's discharge letter before their eyes.

"We did our best." He continued. "The Young Pretender'd not dare turn up here. He knows we don't have any truck with him and his ilk."

Behind him stood Lachie and his band, kitted out proudly in their stolen Redcoat uniforms.

"Aye!" Lachie said. "We're loyal to wee Georgie!"

The Redcoat looked doubtful, but he said nothing.

Maggie slipped away. In the kitchen, she helped herself to some bread and smoked salmon. Then she went out by the stable door, telling the Redcoat posted there that she was going to get some chickens to cook for their dinner.

Lachie followed her outside. "I'm off to lead a search party," he said happily. Then he saw the worried look on her face.

Maggie said nothing.

"It's Charlie, isn't it?" he whispered.

Maggie nodded. "He's heading for Skye."

"Good luck," Lachie said. "I'll try to head them off. You know the glen better than anyone."

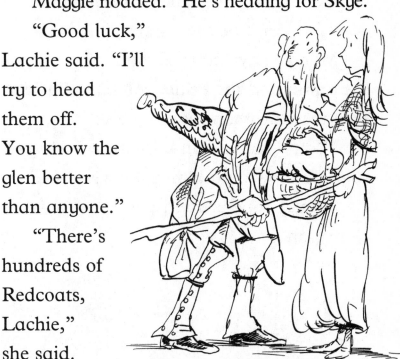

"There's hundreds of Redcoats, Lachie," she said.

Lachie thought for a moment. "Yes, but they're not looking for a woman," he said.

Maggie walked back towards the forest. The Prince and the clansman weren't where she'd left them. She panicked for a moment, until she heard a rustle and the clansman came out from behind a bush where they'd been hiding.

"You can't be too careful," he said.

Maggie gave him the food. The clansman and the Prince ate hungrily and then the clansman rose to leave.

"You'd better wait until dusk," Maggie said. "I know a path they'll never find."

"I only hope you're right," said the clansman.

5

Over the Sea to Skye

As the sun began to slip down towards
the hills, Maggie went on horseback to
check that the path was safe. On her
way back she rode straight into a party
of Redcoats fanned out in a wide line,
searching the forest.

"Halt!" one of the soldiers roared, raising his musket threateningly. Maggie pulled the reins and the horse stopped.

"Where are you heading?" the Redcoat asked her.

Maggie said nothing, her mind churning as the Redcoat shouted to his officer that he had found someone.

"She's just a girl," the officer said.

"Aye," said the soldier in the thick accent of the Scottish Lowlands, "but what's she doing out alone when there's a war on?"

The officer stared at Maggie. "Well," he asked, "what *are* you doing?"

Maggie gulped. Because she was the chief's daughter, she couldn't pretend that she didn't understand English. Briefly, she wondered if she could persuade them that she was deaf.

She took a deep breath. "My mother's cooking dinner for you at the castle," she said. "She told me to tell you it'll be ready soon."

The officer said nothing.

"We're Glenaffin MacDonnells," Maggie said, beginning to panic. "Our men fought with you."

"Is that no' yon bunch of rogues that  burnt our dinners back at Derby?" the soldier asked.

"Maybe," Maggie said sweetly. "That's why my mother's cooking your dinner tonight."

The soldier glowered at her. The officer thought for a moment and then told her to go and tell her mother they would be back within the hour, once another search party had taken their place.

Maggie fled before they changed their minds.

Because of the Redcoats, they couldn't wait for dusk. Maggie led the clansman and the Prince over the hills to the Sound of Sleat. By late afternoon, they were standing a few minutes' walk from the shore. In the distance, they could see the proud rise of the Cuillin Hills of Skye. There, by the shore, a woman was waiting in a boat, ready to row the Prince across the sea.

Neither the clansman nor the Prince had said anything during the journey.

"We'll be safe now," the clansman said. "Thank you."

Maggie smiled and wished them well.

The clansman nodded.

The Prince took Maggie's hand. "Please," he said, "tell your people I'm sorry."

Maggie thought of the men who'd lost their lives, and those who'd been injured. The Prince's apology was no help to them, but they would not want him to die as well.

"Wait," she said, remembering what Lachie'd said.

"What is it?" the clansman asked her.

"I'll give the Prince my skirt and shawl. He's not much taller than me and he's thin. The Redcoats aren't looking for a woman."

"And what'll you wear?"

"I'll make a skirt of his plaid."

Behind a bush, Maggie took her clothes off and shyly handed them to the clansman, who gave her the Prince's plaid and breeches in return.

"For heaven's sake," he said, "hide them. If the Redcoats find you with his breeches, they'll have your head."

They parted then. When she reached the top of the hill Maggie stopped and looked back. The boat was heading for Skye, rowed by the woman Maggie had seen by the shore. Another woman sat in the stern. The Prince, at least, was safe.

When Maggie got home, her father was cursing the Redcoats for having the cheek to demand to be fed.

"Ach," Lachie said, "at least if they're eating, they're not out tormenting people."

Maggie smiled but said nothing.

As night fell, the Redcoats searched with torches, convinced that Charlie was somewhere in the glen.

The chief paced the castle, furious but unable to do anything.

It was then that Maggie told him what had happened. Robby and Neil listened in amazement.

"But you're not with Charlie," Neil said when she finished. "I never said that. I just said I don't believe in war, and I still don't."

"I don't believe you," Robby said, scowling at her.

"I can prove it," Maggie said, lifting her skirt to show them that underneath she wore the Prince's breeches.

◆

Charlie escaped safely to France, although the Redcoats stayed in the Highlands for many months looking for him. When the last of them had gone, the chief took the

Prince's breeches and put them in a frame of burnished oak.

For ever afterwards, the Prince's breeches were proudly displayed on the wall of the Great Hall of the castle, to prove that the MacDonnells had been loyal to the cause after all.

Bonnie Prince Charlie 1720-1788

Charles Edward Stuart was
called Bonnie Prince Charlie or
the Young Pretender, depending
upon which side you were on.
(Charlie's supporters called
King George 'The Usurper').
Charlie was the son of the exiled
King James. He came to Scotland
at the age of twenty-five to lead
a rising. At first the rising was successful. The
Prince arrived in Edinburgh with his Jacobite troops
and his father James, the Old Pretender, was
proclaimed King of England, Scotland, France and
Ireland. But King James VIII never took his throne.
Charles was badly advised, and the invasion of
England was a disaster. Many of Charles's Scottish
supporters deserted him, and the rising was finally
defeated in April 1746 at the Battle of Drummossie
Moor, better known as Culloden. With the help of
many brave Highlanders, Charles managed to
escape to France.

Flora Macdonald 1722–1790

Two months after Culloden, Bonnie Prince Charlie was hiding in South Uist, with government troops in hot pursuit. Flora rowed the Prince, who was disguised as a maid, to Skye. The Prince escaped, but Flora was arrested and held in the Tower of London for a year. The famous Skye Boat Song, 'Over the Sea to Skye', was written to commemorate the escapade.

The Jacobites

The supporters of the Stuart kings were called Jacobites, after Jacobus, the Latin word for James. Although there were Jacobites throughout Great Britain and Ireland, most of them were Scottish Highlanders.

The 'White Cockade' – a white feather pinned to a beret – was the Jacobite symbol.

Highland dress

Although no one is sure about the origins of tartan, it has existed in Scotland for many centuries. But tartan was not used to distinguish the different Highland clans until the late seventeenth and early eighteenth centuries.

Tartan has always been used for the main items of Highland dress – the plaid and the kilt. The plaid was a very versatile garment. It was made from a length of material which was gathered at the waist by a belt and then fastened over the shoulder. The kilt was a much later development which needed less material.

After Culloden the wearing of Highland dress was outlawed by the English. But the Highland regiments were allowed to wear their traditional uniforms and this helped to ensure that tartan is still worn today.